RSPCA

Animal  Tales

Race to the Finish

Other books in the
RSPCA ANIMAL TALES series

Race to the
Finish

David Harding

RANDOM HOUSE AUSTRALIA

A Random House book
Published by Random House Australia Pty Ltd
Level 3, 100 Pacific Highway, North Sydney NSW 2060
www.randomhouse.com.au

First published by Random House Australia in 2012

Addresses for companies within the Random House Group can be
found at www.randomhouse.com.au/offices.

National Library of Australia Cataloguing-in-Publication entry

Author: Harding, David
Title: Race to the finish/David Harding
ISBN: 978 1 74275 342 3 (pbk)
Series: Animal tales; 8
Target Audience: For primary school age
Subjects: Greyhound racing – Juvenile fiction
Dewey Number: A823.4

Cover photograph © addimage/iStockphoto
Cover and internal design by Ingrid Kwong
Internal illustrations by Charlotte Whitby
Internal photographs: image of cat by iStockphoto;
image of horse by Lenkadan/Shutterstock; image of greyhound by
addimage/iStockphoto
Typeset by Midland Typesetters, Australia
Printed in Australia by Griffin Press, an accredited ISO AS/NZS
14001:2004 Environmental Management System printer

Random House Australia uses papers that are natural, renewable
and recyclable products and made from wood grown in sustainable
forests. The logging and manufacturing processes are expected to
conform to the environmental regulations of the country of origin.

Chapter One

Ben Stoppard's voice boomed around the park. 'Welcome, ladies and gentlemen, to the Abbotts Hill Games!'

His friend Cassie Bannerman laughed. 'This is silly,' she said with a shake of her head. 'Now I wish I hadn't said I would challenge you.'

She looped her dog Ripper's leash around a wooden post that held a bubbler. Ripper yapped and began jumping around her feet.

'Easy, boy,' Cassie said, giving Ripper a scratch behind the ear just where he liked it. 'This won't take long.' Then she winked at Ripper so Ben couldn't see. 'You just watch me win!'

Ripper barked happily as if cheering Cassie on. Ben came over to the bubbler and secured his own dog. Florence, a large shaggy Old English sheepdog, began barking happily with her best friend, Ripper.

'Who will win the battle of Abbotts Hill?' Ben continued. 'Two of the world's greatest nine-and-a-half-year-old athletes are on the field and ready to go!'

Cassie chuckled again. 'So what's first? Long jump, hurdles or shot-put?'

Ben's eyes narrowed as he ran all the events he could think of through his mind. Ever since he was sick the day of the school athletics carnival he had wanted to prove himself. And who better to challenge than Cassie – the best athlete in year five.

Ben looked down. He was still holding the frisbee they had been throwing for Florence and Ripper just minutes before.

'How about discus?' said Ben.

'Fine,' said Cassie. 'Furthest throw wins.'

'The first event on today's program,' said Ben, curving his hands around his mouth like a megaphone, 'is discus.' He waved the frisbee in the air, making Florence and

Ripper jump around excitedly. 'The crowd is going wild!'

Cassie turned to the dogs. 'Sit,' she commanded.

Ben watched Ripper sit up straight and rigid while Florence rolled over, her legs in the air. For the hundredth time the difference between Florence and Ripper was all too obvious. But it didn't bother Ben; he loved his dog no matter what.

'Okay, let's get this over with,' said Cassie. 'I help in the deli on Friday afternoons, remember?'

'Ladies first.'

Cassie took the frisbee and faced away from the dogs towards a large grassed area of the park. She pulled back on her arm and then curled the frisbee through the air like a slingshot. It flew straight and fast before curving, lowering and landing in the grass.

Ben swallowed. Cassie had thrown it a lot further than he had expected. He jogged away to get the frisbee and put a large piece of bark in its place. Then Ben walked all the way back to the bubbler, where Cassie waited triumphantly.

'Think you can beat that?' she asked.

'Sure,' said Ben, 'no problem.'

Florence barked in agreement. Ben took some deep breaths. Then he released the frisbee with a grunt.

All four pairs of eyes followed the yellow disc as it span and flew through the air. It was getting close to the bark marker, but it was beginning to turn. Ben tightened his fists.

Come on, you can make it!

But then something blurred across the grass like an arrow shot from a bow. A creature – black and galloping – leapt into the air and took the frisbee into its mouth while it was still a couple of metres off the ground.

Cassie and Ben ran towards their frisbee and whatever it was that had caught it. They froze.

A tall boy had walked in front of them. Ben recognised him from school and knew he was in year six. But the boy wasn't the reason they had stopped running. Ben and Cassie stood, staring at what was at the end of the lead in the boy's hand.

'Well, that's the most magnificent-looking dog I've ever seen,' said Cassie.

7

Chapter Two

'Sorry we interrupted your game,' said the boy, patting his dog, 'but Rocket loves running. And catching things.'

Ben and Cassie just looked at Rocket, then at each other.

'That's okay,' said Cassie. 'We were just pretending we were at the Olympics.'

'Rocket's an athlete,' said the boy, 'a racing greyhound. She's probably won more medals than you two ever will.'

'Wow,' said Ben.

This was a dog that looked like no other. Standing tall and alert, Rocket seemed more like a statue from a museum than a pet. She was taller than Florence and Ripper, and more than half the height of Ben. Her hair was short and a lovely deep black that shone in the sun. Her face, legs and tail were all long and strong, and reminded Ben of a small horse.

'I've seen you guys at school,' said the boy. 'My name's Craig Stephenson.'

Ben and Cassie hardly heard him. 'Can we pat her?' they asked together.

Craig laughed. 'Dad doesn't usually let our greyhounds get stroked by others, but

Rocket's retired from racing now. Knock yourself out.'

Cassie and Ben gave Rocket a pat all over. She clearly loved it!

'Are those your dogs over there?' Craig asked, pointing at a multicoloured ball of fur near the bubbler. Florence and Ripper were having a great time wrestling again. Rocket was their opposite, still standing to attention. Ben reckoned her obedience might even put Ripper to shame.

Craig and Rocket walked Ben and Cassie to their dogs. Once Florence and Ripper had their leads unhooked from the bubbler they tugged on them, trying to get closer to Rocket.

Ben laughed. 'It seems they like Rocket as much as we do!'

'I can't blame them,' said Craig. 'As I said, Rocket doesn't race anymore, so she's allowed to make new friends.'

'By the way, my name is Ben and this is Cassie.'

Cassie was standing at a distance, watching her dog get acquainted with Rocket. Ben was confused. Usually Cassie was the first person to introduce herself.

He turned back to Craig. 'I like your dog's lead,' Ben said to him.

Rocket's lead was bright green and stood out against Florence's tatty old black one.

'Rocket has to have this lead whenever I take her out,' said Craig. 'It means she has been through a special training program and cleared to walk without a muzzle.'

Ben knew what a muzzle was – a mask

that's normally attached around the dog's snout. Ben hated them. He thought they looked like cages.

'Does that mean greyhounds bite?' he asked.

'I have never heard of a greyhound biting a person,' said Cassie from behind Ben. 'There are lots of myths about them.'

'That's right,' said Craig. 'You really know your animals! Greyhounds make great pets.'

Ben already knew Cassie was the number-one animal expert in town. She knew loads more about pets than Ben did, and his dad was a vet at the RSPCA!

But Ben also knew Cassie well enough to realise she was upset about something, and that worried him.

Chapter Three

'Come on, Ripper, we should get going,' said Cassie after a moment of silence.

'We have to run too,' said Craig. He turned to leave with Rocket but then stopped. 'Hey,' he said, 'would you like to see greyhound racing at the track tomorrow? I'll be there with my dad. I can show you around.'

Ben didn't have to think about it. 'Sure!' he said.

'I have to work in my family's deli,' answered Cassie.

It sounded to Ben as if she didn't want to go anyway.

'That's okay,' said Craig. 'Ben, meet me outside Abbotts Park Racetrack at noon. But leave your dog at home, she won't be allowed in.'

Ben nodded vigorously. 'I'll be there,' he said, trying not to look at Florence's drooping face and ears. 'I can't wait!'

Ben stood motionless with Florence, watching their new friends walk away. It was a minute before he noticed Cassie was gone.

Ben trotted up the street after her. 'Hey,

wait up!' he called. 'I'll walk home with you.'

'Okay,' was all Cassie said.

'So, what do you think?' asked Ben.

'About what?'

'Craig,' said Ben. 'He's so cool, and his dog is a beauty!'

'Well, that is true. Greyhounds are stunning animals.'

Ben swallowed. Something was definitely up. They turned the corner into Cassie's street. 'Don't you like Craig?' he asked.

Cassie didn't speak for a moment. 'I don't know . . .' she said. 'Don't you think it was strange when Craig said his dad didn't like people patting their dogs? They don't seem to want their pets socialising.'

Now it was Ben's turn to be quiet. Deep down he knew Cassie was right. But then he remembered Craig's invitation to go out tomorrow. Craig seemed to like Ben and he had found it hard making friends since moving to Abbotts Hill – except for Cassie, of course.

'Look,' he said, 'I know that what Craig said sounded strange, but he seems nice. And besides, why would his family own dogs if they didn't like them?'

Cassie sighed. They had stopped in front of the deli. Cassie's mum called out to them from inside the shop. Ben and Cassie waved lazily back at her.

'I think you need to speak to your dad,' she said, looking down. 'He'll be able to show you better than I can tell you.'

Cassie walked into the shop with Ripper at her heels. He gave a 'goodbye' bark to Florence and Ben.

Something is definitely wrong with her, thought Ben.

His eyes fell on Cassie's cat, Gladiator, who was normally full of beans but today preferred lazing about in his basket, underneath a spot of sunshine.

Then Ben watched Cassie take up her familiar place behind the counter. There, she lovingly stroked Gladiator's soft fur as he slept in his basket.

Ben's mouth tightened. Cassie had been a great friend. It would be sad if she and Craig couldn't get on, but why should that stop *him*? He turned away, stomping off towards his own house with Florence in tow.

Chapter Four

The next day was Saturday. That meant two things for Ben: no school and the chance to see his first greyhound race. When he'd told his dad about his new friend, Dr Joe was really pleased. He became less so when Ben spoke of the greyhound race.

'But I met Craig's dog Rocket and he loves dogs like I do, Dad,' said Ben.

'That may be so, Ben,' replied Dr Joe, 'but you may find there isn't a lot of respect for greyhounds at the track.'

Ben didn't want to miss out. 'Well, I'd like to see for myself. And Craig's dad will be there to keep an eye on us.'

'You mean Alan Stephenson? I think we've met before at the Bannermans' deli. Seems like a nice guy . . .' Dr Joe paused before sighing. 'Okay, son, you take a look at what goes on and we can have a chat about it later.'

Ben gave Florence a goodbye pat and headed out the door.

The racetrack was only a short walk away, next to the train line that stretched away into the city. As Ben approached it he could hear a voice on a loudspeaker announcing races as a crowd cheered. He wondered how fast and exciting a greyhound race actually was.

'Ben! Hey, Ben!' called Craig, waving. He was waiting for Ben outside the race with his dad.

Ben smiled and ran up to them. 'Hi,' he said.

'It was great you could come,' said Craig. 'It'll be fun! Dad, this is my friend Ben.'

'Hi Ben, nice to meet you.' Craig's dad had a gruff voice but a kind face. He offered his hand out for Ben to shake.

'Hi Mr Stephenson,' Ben replied, taking his hand and shaking it.

As the trio walked towards the exciting noises, Ben looked up at the large, brick-wall entranceway with the words 'Abbotts Park Racetrack' written near the top in old, metal letters. Ben followed Craig and his dad along the wall, past the ticket window to a set of turnstiles.

A man standing in a neon yellow vest stopped to greet them. 'Looking forward to seeing how Slipstream goes today,' he said with a tip of his hat.

'Fingers crossed, Rick,' Mr Stephenson responded with a smile.

Craig turned to Ben. 'Slipstream's our contender. Dad's been training her really hard.'

Ben nodded, still taking in the activities and the atmosphere of the busy racetrack.

The metal turnstile clicked as first Mr Stephenson, Craig, and then Ben passed through it. Ben found himself in an area with places to buy food. In front of him, a short hill sloped downwards towards a circular race track. The track at the bottom was made of dirt with high metal fences running along either side of it. Trainers with their kennels full of dogs were gathered in a grassed oval inside the track.

'Awaiting starter's orders,' said the announcer. The group quickly found a seat on one of the benches that were strung around the hill slope. '... And they're off!'

There was a loud beep and a flash of lights. On the track in front of Ben a small row of boxes crashed open and a line of muzzled greyhounds shot out of them. Immediately they began bounding along the racetrack, faster than Ben's dad drove the car.

Ben's jaw dropped. 'Wow, they're much quicker than I expected,' he said. 'How do they know where to run?'

'They're chasing the mechanical rabbit, see?' Craig pointed to the track. A little way in front of the lead dog was a small cloth rabbit whizzing along the top rail of the inside fence.

Already the dogs were rounding the last turn on the track. People were shouting and cheering. Craig and his dad stood up enthusiastically. 'C'mon, Slipstream!' they called.

A light brown dog was picking

up speed and moving up between the first- and second-placed dogs. As the pack crossed the finish line, the crowd cheered.

'Yeah, Slipstream!' shouted Craig. 'He won! He's our current champion, maybe even better than Rocket.'

Spectators came over and began patting

Mr Stephenson on the back and saying things like, 'well done' and 'great job'.

Craig's father turned to the boys. 'I'm going to pick up Slipstream. You kids come down when you're ready.'

'Okay, Dad.' Craig looked on at his father with pride.

Ben smiled. It felt good to watch his new friend win.

As Ben clapped, he watched the trainers collect their amazing dogs from the track. He could see Mr Stephenson running up towards Slipstream, who was panting like a steam engine inside her muzzle. Then, a few metres away from her, one of the other greyhounds collapsed.

'Hey!' Ben shouted.

He waited for someone to help the dog.

No one did. He tugged on Craig's sleeve, but he was too busy talking to his adult friends about the race.

The dog wore a blue apron with a big number one printed on it that was heaving up and down with the dog's chest. Ben's eyes were glued to the greyhound as it struggled to catch its breath. Eventually one of the race officials squatted over the dog, covering Ben's view of it.

Something about this feels very wrong, thought Ben.

Maybe Cassie had been right.

Chapter Five

Ben walked home slowly that afternoon. He stopped at Cassie's deli along the way. From outside he heard the cash register close as Cassie said, 'Say hello to Cuddles for me, Mrs P.'

Mrs Papandrea, Ben's neighbour, turned to leave the shop and almost tripped over Ben as he walked inside. 'Sorry, Mrs P,' he said.

She grunted and walked out.

'Hi, Ben,' said Cassie, straightening some packets of spaghetti on a shelf. 'How was the race?'

'Okay, I guess,' he said. 'It was exciting.'

'Uh-huh.'

'But it was a bit weird, too.'

'How do you mean?' she asked.

'Well, I'm not sure all the dogs are being treated well by their trainers,' said Ben.

Cassie stopped moving pasta around aimlessly.

'I like Craig,' Ben continued. 'And it was good of him to invite me out with his dad. I mean, since moving here I haven't made any friends except for you.'

A familiar 'yap-yap!' came from behind the counter. Ben looked over and saw Ripper dozing on a mat near Gladiator. 'Sorry, Ripper, you're my friend too.'

Cassie laughed.

'Craig invited me to go to his house tomorrow after lunch,' said Ben.

'That's nice,' said Cassie. 'While you're there you could see how they treat their greyhounds with your own eyes.'

'I'm sure there's nothing to worry about,' said Ben. 'But, just in case, would you like to come too?'

'Definitely,' Cassie said and smiled.

That night, Ben's dad, Dr Joe Stoppard, was watching leftovers rotate inside their humming microwave. 'Oh, I forgot to ask you,' he said, 'how was the greyhound racing with Craig and his dad?'

'Fine,' said Ben, running his fingers through Florence's shaggy fur as he waited for dinner.

'What did Cassie think?'

'She didn't go,' said Ben. He began to work on Florence's neck and ears. 'Well, Cassie wouldn't have liked it anyway,' he added. 'She is *not* a big fan of greyhound racing.'

'Hmm . . . that's what I figured.' Dr Joe took the plate out of the microwave. 'Still not hot enough.'

'Cassie seemed to think you wouldn't like greyhound racing either,' said Ben.

Ben's dad put the plate back in the microwave. 'I work with the RSPCA,' he said. 'So unfortunatly I see some worrying things about greyhound racing.'

Ben and Florence looked up with their eyes wide open. 'What do you mean?' asked Ben.

'We'll eat later,' said Dr Joe as he put the leftovers back in the fridge. 'I think I need to show you something.'

Ben and his dad walked to the RSPCA shelter. After unlocking the door, his dad led Ben past the front counter and vet clinic, down a passage to where Ben knew the animals waiting for adoption were housed.

'Hi, Jen,' said Ben's dad to the vet nurse, who was feeding some cats in their cages. 'We're just here to visit our new arrival.'

Jen saluted as they walked towards the corridor. Ben waved back and called out hello to a few of the animals as he passed by. There were a few meows in reply.

Ben and Dr Joe continued down a passageway until they entered a separate room, where Ben's dad stopped in front of a large enclosure. He put his hands on his hips and peered into it. 'She's lovely, isn't she?' he said.

Ben looked through the wire door. A black greyhound with a white line running down her face was sitting in the corner.

Ben squatted down and said hello. The dog looked up but didn't move.

'She was found roaming the streets,' said his dad. 'Greyhounds only race until they are five or six years old – if they're lucky. Most trainers can't afford to keep all their non-running dogs as pets.'

'But dogs live at least ten years,' said Ben. 'Where do all the greyhounds go after racing?'

'There are adoption programs. And we do our best to find foster homes for unwanted greyhounds, though it isn't easy.'

Ben stood up. 'But what happens to all the retired dogs that aren't found?'

His dad shook his head. 'The truth is, we don't know.'

Chapter Six

The next day Ben and Cassie were welcomed into Craig's living room. There, Rocket was draped over a sofa, half asleep and clearly very happy. It surprised Ben how calm and relaxed greyhounds seemed to be when they weren't chasing mechanical rabbits around a racetrack.

'Well, you know who the boss of this house is,' Cassie said and laughed. She gave Rocket a friendly rub.

Craig chuckled. 'Yeah, she's the happiest animal I've ever met. We love her heaps.'

Ben and Cassie smiled at each other. Maybe things weren't as bad as they thought.

Craig's father entered the room and shook both Ben's and Cassie's hands.

'Dad, you've already met Ben, but this is Cassie. She goes to the same school as us, and she fell in love with Rocket too,' said Craig.

'Well, who wouldn't?' said his dad. 'You know, before Rocket I didn't realise greyhounds made such great pets.'

'But Mr Stephenson,' Cassie asked, 'you own a lot of greyhounds, don't you?'

'We sure do! Racing has been in this family for three generations now. Why don't you come outside and meet the gang?'

The four of them walked out the back door. Outside, the Stephensons had a large yard that contained a wide grassy area in front of their own miniature racetrack.

'Over there is where we train the dogs,' said Craig. 'Here is where we house them.'

Ben looked around. He couldn't see any dogs except for Rocket, who had followed them outside. Then he noticed rows of tiny kennels along the back of the house. Each one was barely large enough to hold a greyhound.

Please don't let there be dogs inside them, he thought.

'Here's Slipstream,' said Mr Stephenson, pointing into the first kennel. 'He only started racing this season and already has three wins.'

Ben and Cassie peered through the grille door. Slipstream stared back from the darkness within.

'He doesn't have a very big dog house,' said Ben.

'Don't worry, he gets plenty of exercise,' said Craig. 'You saw him run yesterday!'

'Some dogs can run over sixty kilometres an hour,' said Mr Stephenson. 'But obviously they can't keep up that sort of speed for long. That's why the races are short.'

Craig's dad was clearly proud of his dogs, but Ben wondered why Rocket was the only greyhound allowed to be loved and not kept in a cage all day.

They walked down the row and Mr Stephenson opened the final cage. A lovely, light-brown greyhound with white feet jumped out and excitedly licked his owner.

Mr Stephenson laughed before saying, 'Meet Dodger. He hasn't won any races, but he's a nice dog. Would you two like to take him home?'

Ben and Cassie were both shocked by the question. 'Sorry, Mr Stephenson,' said Cassie, 'we already own dogs.'

'That's a shame,' Craig's dad replied. 'We can't afford to keep him anymore. I'll give him one more chance to win. Then his time is up.'

Cassie tightened. She stood tall. 'I'm sorry, Mr Stephenson, but this isn't fair at all. These dogs deserve a better life.'

'Nonsense,' he said. 'You should see them race. They love it!'

Ben looked along the rows of majestic dogs locked in their tiny cages and wondered.

Chapter Seven

Ben and Cassie couldn't walk home fast enough. They picked up Florence and Ripper before heading to the park so that the dogs could run around in the wide, open spaces.

Watching their canine friends chase after frisbees and each other, Ben's mind kept returning to the Stephensons' dogs.

'You were right, you know,' said Ben. 'It isn't fair on the greyhounds.'

'I've been thinking about what Craig's dad said,' commented Cassie, 'and I don't think it matters whether or not the dogs like racing. They don't deserve to be locked up.'

'Or being thrown away after they lose a few races,' added Ben. 'There's an abandoned greyhound at the RSPCA right now.'

'I know,' said Cassie. 'I found it one day after school a few weeks ago.'

Ripper dropped his yellow frisbee at Cassie's feet. She threw it across the grass for him again. 'At least we can be good friends to our dogs,' she said.

Ben knew that was true but he wanted to do more. He didn't like the idea of greyhounds being no longer wanted. But what could he do?

Florence raced up to Ben and jumped on him, barking happily. Ben fell backwards before Ripper jumped on top of them both. Ben laughed as he struggled onto his feet.

'You know, I think that Craig and his dad like dogs just as much as we do,' said Cassie. 'They both told us Rocket was a great pet. They just have to stop seeing their other dogs as objects.'

'And how do we teach them that?' asked Ben. He had just finished brushing off his pants when Florence and Ripper jumped up on his legs again. All three fell backwards for the second time.

'I don't know,' Cassie replied, chuckling.

'But I have a feeling we're just the sort of people who could help them see a better way.'

Chapter Eight

The next day after school Ben went straight to the RSPCA. He couldn't get the homeless greyhound out of his mind. She was still there, sitting in the same corner of the kennel.

Jen the vet nurse came up behind Ben and sighed. 'It's sad, isn't it?' she said. 'She has a lot of time in the exercise yard, but she doesn't move around much in here.'

'Why?' asked Ben.

'Apparently greyhounds are often kept in tiny kennels. Sometimes they can't forget what living in one is like, even when they have more room.'

'Has anyone wanted to take her home yet?' asked Ben with his fingers crossed.

'Most people that come to adopt a pet want a puppy or a kitten. It's tricky finding the right homes for older animals that have had a hard life.'

'But greyhounds make great pets,' said Ben.

'Tell me about it,' said Jen. 'I've already adopted two greyhounds. They're great fun and so easy-going. But I can't take every animal we find home.'

Ben heard something scratch at the enclosure's connecting wall. He leaned around to check who might be living next door.

'Oh,' said Jen, 'that's a new greyhound who's just come into the main shelter today. It seems his owner no longer wanted him.'

Ben looked in. A bouncing, gorgeous greyhound with light-brown fur yapped at him. The dog was the same colour as Dodger from the Stephensons' house the day before.

I hope none of Craig's dogs have been left unwanted and had to be rescued by the RSPCA, thought Ben. He patted the dog as best as he could, slotting his fingers through the square holes in the wire door. 'Good boy.'

Some familiar-sounding footsteps echoed between the rows of kennels. Ben turned to see his dad walking down the passageway. A tall, familiar boy walked beside him.

'Craig!' called Ben.

'Hi, I was walking Rocket and saw you come inside. I've been chatting to your dad. He said he might come by and give our dogs a check-up sometime.'

Ben's dad nodded. 'I'd be happy to. Anyway, we'll leave Ben to show you around. Call out if you need us.'

Dr Joe and Jen left the boys to care for an injured kitten that had been brought in.

'So who's living in here, then?' asked Craig. Ben was doing his best to hide the large kennels behind him as Craig tried to look inside.

'Um . . .' was all Ben could say. Slowly he moved aside to let his new friend see.

'Greyhounds?' gasped Craig. 'What on earth are they doing here?'

'The RSPCA finds lots of greyhounds each year,' said Ben. 'Some trainers don't have any use for them once their racing days are over.'

'But . . . *why?* My dad says he always tries to find families for our dogs,' said Craig. 'He wouldn't leave them that way.'

'Your dad's a nice guy,' said Ben, 'I'm sure he doesn't. But somehow I don't think there are enough families for all the retired dogs out there.'

Craig frowned. He watched the dogs for a long time, saying nothing. Finally he walked closer to the cage of the quiet greyhound. 'Girl,' he whispered. 'Hiya, girl!'

The dog stood up and came over to Craig, curious.

'I never thought it could end like this,' said Craig. 'When you think about it, I'm not sure many greyhounds have much of a life, from beginning to end.'

'It doesn't have to be this way,' said Ben. They stood together, stroking the dogs through the doors with their fingertips. 'I know I'd rather be happy and come second than be miserable and win.'

Craig stood up, his mouth tight and his

fists clenched. 'Let's tell your dad to get the adoption paperwork ready,' he said. 'I'm going to get Dad to bring these dogs home.'

Chapter Nine

Five minutes later Ben and Craig collected Rocket from the front of the RSPCA and started for Craig's house. On the way, the boys stopped at Ben's house to collect Florence, who was overjoyed to walk beside Rocket. She and Craig seemed happy too. Watching them, Ben wanted to believe that Rocket enjoyed being treated as a pet much more than as a racer.

Mrs Papandrea was weeding her garden as they walked down Ben's driveway and up the street. A dash of cat fur across her lawn suggested Cuddles was not interested in meeting any greyhounds.

'Hi, Mrs P,' called Ben as they passed her fence.

'Cuddles!' she cried. 'You scared my poor Cuddles away with your big dog.'

Mrs P stood up to give the boys a talking to when her eyes fell on Rocket as she strutted along the footpath.

'Well, I never!' she gasped. 'What a lovely dog. Can I pat her?'

'Yes!' said Craig and Ben together.

They laughed. Ben had never seen

Mrs P so happy to spend time with him – or a dog. She kept watching the boys and their pets as they walked up the street towards Cassie's house.

'Your neighbour seems nice,' said Craig.

'Well, I guess she is – when greyhounds are around,' said Ben.

As they approached Cassie's shop she jumped out of the deli with Ripper. 'I thought I heard you two coming,' she said. 'Going for a walk?'

'We're on the way to Craig's,' said Ben. 'Want to come?'

Cassie looked at Rocket. Then her eyes followed the dog's lead up to Craig's smiling face. 'Sure,' she said. 'You two are up to something, aren't you?'

'Not really,' said Ben.

'But it would be great if you could come along,' added Craig. 'We need your help to talk to my dad.'

'About what?' she asked.

'Remember how you said the way we treated dogs wasn't fair? Well, I think I agree with you now.'

'He wants his dad to adopt some dogs at the RSPCA,' said Ben.

Cassie beamed. She joined them in their walk to Craig's house: three friends with three happy dogs.

But when they stopped to cross a road, Craig froze. 'Oh no, I just remembered! Dad's not home. He'll be at the Monday-night races at Abbott Park.'

Ben and Cassie groaned. 'I guess we'll just have to do it tomorrow,' said Ben.

'No, we have to go,' said Craig, beginning to jog, 'tonight.'

'What's up?' asked Cassie. 'Why the rush?'

'I've just realised,' said Craig with wide eyes. 'Dodger! Dad said if he didn't run well tonight we couldn't afford to keep him anymore. I didn't think anything of it at the time, but now –'

Ben interrupted. 'Do you think if we don't get there . . .?' He let his question hang in the air.

'I hope not,' said Craig, 'I never thought he would do something like that. But now I'm not so sure . . .'

'C'mon,' said Cassie, 'stop talking! We have to get there before it's too late!'

Chapter Ten

Rocket showed what great runners grey-hounds are. She had very soon pulled Craig to the front of the group, leaving Cassie and Ben a close second and third behind them.

Ben looked at Florence as she ran along the footpath in front of him. Her tongue was almost hanging out as she bounded along. Ben thought that if dogs could smile she was definitely doing it now.

'I . . . *puff* . . . have to admit that I don't have any idea . . . *puff* . . . what we're going to do when we get there,' Ben said to Cassie as they ran.

'We have to . . . *huff* . . . try to do something,' she answered over her shoulder.

Ben knew they could not afford to be late. Craig had told them that the race was scheduled for five o'clock. If they didn't hurry they would miss the chance to find Craig's dad before he might 'get rid' of Dodger.

They stopped once or twice, when they had to cross a road, and Ben took the opportunity to gulp as much air into his lungs as he could. 'This running is unbearable,' he said to himself. 'I don't know how dogs keep it up.'

By the time they arrived at the racetrack it was one minute to five. 'Just in time,' said Ben. There was a tap outside the track entrance with an old ice-cream container full of water beneath it. After all three dogs had taken some refreshing gulps, Craig, Cassie and Ben looked at each other.

'So how do we get inside?' asked Cassie.

'Leave that to me,' answered Craig. 'Our dogs won't be allowed in, though. They'll distract the runners.'

It was then that Ben heard the familiar sounds that meant the race had begun. 'Quick!' he said, tying Florence's leash to the tap. The others tied their dogs up too

and ran through the entrance to Abbotts
Park.

Just in time to see Dodger finish fourth.

'Oh, great,' groaned Craig. 'And he's such a good dog.'

They watched Dodger's light-brown outline and white feet walk around the track as he caught his breath. Craig's dad appeared. He stood over his dog, shaking his head, before taking off Dodger's blue apron with the number seven on it.

Ben looked at Craig. His cheeks were red and he was shaking his head too. 'It's not fair,' he muttered.

Cassie snapped to attention. 'C'mon, we need to talk to your dad. How do we get down there?'

'I'm not sure we can get to Dad that way,' he answered. 'Besides, I have a better idea.'

Chapter Eleven

Craig ran back outside to where the dogs were tied up. Puzzled, Ben and Cassie followed him. Their three dogs barked happily, realising their time without their owners was a short one. Unhooking their pets, Ben and Cassie followed Craig around the outside of Abbotts Park.

Abbotts Park's front brick wall was soon replaced by a wire fence that encircled the entire arena. Through the fence they watched Craig's dad take Dodger from the racetrack area and disappear behind some small buildings.

'They've gone to the trainer's car park and exit,' said Craig as he was dragged along by Rocket. 'Run!'

'Oh no, not more running,' said Ben.

'Stop whingeing,' Cassie said and smiled. 'This is one race we have to see through to the finish.'

Huffing and puffing, they made it around to the back entrance. They ran inside and scanned the car park for any sign of Craig's dad or Dodger.

'There!' said Cassie.

A white van was parked under a tree. On the side of the van was written: 'Stephenson's Greyhounds.' In the back, Ben and Cassie could see a number of small kennels, each holding a tightly packed greyhound. Craig's dad then appeared from the other side of the van carrying an empty kennel. He placed it inside the van and slammed the back doors.

'Dad!' called Craig. 'Why is Dodger's kennel empty?'

Mr Stephenson spun around. 'What are you lot doing here?' he asked.

Before Craig could answer, Rocket began barking loudly. Then, from outside the Abbotts Park fence, another dog joined in. Everyone turned around to see a light-brown greyhound run up the driveway, barking all the way.

'It's Dodger!' said Ben.

Dodger ran straight to Craig and Rocket. The two greyhounds began yapping and rubbing their faces against each other. Florence and Ripper joined in too. Other trainers who were packing up their own vans looked on in surprise.

Craig looped Dodger's lead through Rocket's collar. He squatted down and put his arms around his two greyhounds.

'This is why I'm here, Dad,' said Craig, 'to take our dogs home. All of them.'

Mr Stephenson lowered his face. 'Craig,' he said quietly, 'I'd like to keep all our dogs, but we can't afford it. You know that.'

'Then we will have to find them all foster families,' said Craig.

'I've said this before,' said Cassie.

'Animals deserve to be treated fairly, just like people do.'

Craig's dad slapped his hand against his forehead. 'What are you kids talking about? Craig, did you actually think I would let go of Dodger that way?'

A man ran up the driveway, hollering all the way. 'Hey, Stephenson,' he called, 'that dog you sold me bolted as I was putting him in my car!'

Ben, Cassie and Craig looked at each other in confusion. Mr Stephenson looked at Craig and sighed. 'This is my friend George. He bought Dodger from me. He's trying to start up his own greyhound-training business.'

Ben blushed and looked away.

George chuckled. 'Looks like old

Dodger here isn't ready to leave you! No harm done – you can have him back.'

Mr Stephenson apologised to his friend and gave the money back.

'Sorry, Dad,' said Craig. 'I should have trusted you.'

'It's fine,' said Mr Stephenson. 'I know there are some uncaring people out there. But I'm doing my best.'

'I know.'

'Speaking of which,' said Cassie, 'what about the dogs at the RSPCA?'

Craig explained to his dad about the two unwanted dogs. Mr Stephenson sighed. 'Get in the van. We'll talk about it on the way home.'

After borrowing a spare kennel for Rocket, all of the Stephensons' dogs were soon loaded into their van. Craig climbed in the front with his dad. Outside, Ben and Cassie watched as Craig's dad shut his door and turned the key in the ignition.

'I still don't like those kennels,' said Ben.

'I know, but I have a feeling things are about to change at the Stephensons' house,' said Cassie.

She waved goodbye at the van as it drove away. Through the windscreen, Ben saw Craig wave back and smile.

Chapter Twelve

A few days later, Ben's voice was echoing around the park once again. 'Welcome back, ladies and gentlemen, to the Abbotts Hill Games!'

Cassie, holding Ripper's lead, put her hands on her hips. 'Wait a minute,' she said, 'I never said I'd challenge you at discus again.'

Ben smiled. 'The competitors have assembled and are ready for their first throws!'

'No, Ben, I don't feel like it, I'm worn out.'

'What's the matter,' asked Ben, 'afraid you'll lose?'

'I don't care whether I win or not,' said Cassie, 'I just –'

She stopped speaking to stare at something in the distance. Ben bent down to pick up the frisbee from where it lay next to Ripper. A rumbling of barking dogs began behind him.

'I didn't know you were helping out with dog-training lessons today,' Ben said.

'I'm not,' said Cassie. 'Look.'

Ben looked up. He hadn't seen Craig

since Monday night. Since then, most of his time had been spent wondering if Craig had persuaded his dad to change the way they treated their dogs. As he watched Craig and his dad enter the park, all of his questions were answered.

The Stephensons were surrounded by eight happily prancing greyhounds on bright green leads.

Ben and Cassie waved to them and Craig waved back. Soon Ripper and Florence were playing happily with Rocket, Dodger and six new friends.

'We've changed the set up at home,' said Craig. 'Plenty of exercise and socialising. Bigger kennels – the lot!'

That made Ben and Cassie feel good.

'And we're thinking of starting up an

adoption agency for retired greyhounds, and later on, we'll be able to help the RSPCA re-home any greyhounds that turn up. Dad called up some more of his friends and asked if they were interested in adopting a greyhound, and the two dogs from the RSPCA have now found a new home.'

Then Mr Stephenson spoke. 'In fact, I'm thinking of changing the name of Stephenson's Greyhound Racing to Stephenson's Greyhound Adoption Agency.'

Ben's jaw dropped.

'It's true,' he said, laughing. 'I just got off the phone with your father, Ben. He gave me some pointers on how to get started.'

'That's my dad,' said Craig, looking prouder than he was when he saw him win at the racetrack the other day. 'Awesome!'

'You have no idea how happy we are to hear all this,' said Cassie.

'We thought you would be,' said Craig.

The four of them stayed at the park all afternoon, throwing frisbees and tennis balls for the dogs.

When it was time for the Stephensons to leave, Ben walked up to Craig's dad. 'Mr Stephenson, I've been thinking. What was it that made you change?'

'That's easy,' he said. 'Something Craig said to me in the van the other night really shook me up.'

'What was it?'

'He asked me a question: If I were in a race, would I rather be happy and come second, or be miserable and win?'

Ben smiled, listening to the greyhounds playing happily on the grass around him. He was pleased that he and Cassie could have made such a difference.

'Greyhounds deserve to be well treated,' said Mr Stephenson, 'from start to finish.'

A short time later, Ben and Cassie were sitting alone in the shade as their dogs dozed beside them.

'I'm glad about the Stephensons, but something about greyhound racing still bothers me,' said Cassie. 'I wish it didn't happen at all.'

Ben nodded. 'One life-changing adventure at a time,' he said, grinning. 'Or you'll wear me out!'

'Well,' said Cassie, 'at least that means you won't challenge me any more –'

'It's time, ladies and gentlemen,' Ben shouted, standing up, 'for the Abbotts Hill Games!'

Ripper and Florence picked up their ears. Cassie flopped backwards into the grass. This was one afternoon she wished she did have to work at the deli.

ABOUT THE RSPCA

The RSPCA is the country's best known and most respected animal welfare organisation. The first RSPCA in Australia was formed in Victoria in 1871, and the organisation is now represented by RSPCAs in every state and territory.

The RSPCA's mission is to prevent cruelty to animals by actively promoting their care and protection. It is a not-for-profit charity that is firmly based in the Australian community, relying upon the support of individuals, businesses and organisations to survive and continue its vital work.

Every year, RSPCA shelters throughout Australia accept over 150,000 sick, injured or abandoned animals from the community. The RSPCA believes that every animal is entitled to the Five Freedoms:

Fact File

- freedom from hunger and thirst (ready access to fresh water and a healthy, balanced diet)
- freedom from discomfort, including accommodation in an appropriate environment that has shelter and a comfortable resting area
- freedom from pain, injury or disease through prevention or rapid diagnosis and providing veterinary treatment when required

- freedom to express normal behaviour, including sufficient space, proper facilities and company of the animal's own kind and
- freedom from fear and distress through conditions and treatment that avoid suffering.

GREYHOUND RESCUE AND ADOPTION

With greyhound racing, as with any sport involving animals, there is the potential for the animals involved to experience poor welfare or suffer injury, pain or distress as a result of training or competition.

Racing greyhounds can become unwanted by their owners because they don't win races, or if they are injured or are too old to compete. Greyhound adoption programs allow for some of these retired greyhounds to find new homes, where they receive the love and attention they need.

Fact File

Why do retired greyhounds make great pets?

- They are generally gentle, affectionate and quiet dogs
- Most greyhounds get along well with other animals, including with smaller dogs and with cats
- They don't have much hair and therefore don't require a lot of grooming
- They don't need a lot of exercise apart from a daily walk
- They generally adapt very quickly to their new life, and most make wonderful family companions

How do I adopt a retired greyhound?

There are many ways to adopt retired greyhounds. First off, it's essential you consider carefully the importance of giving a once-working greyhound a new home by providing a well-fenced yard, regular exercise and company.

Fact File

Most states also have their own greyhound adoption program, which aims to rescue and re-home retired or unwanted racing greyhounds. You can find out more about adopting retired greyhounds by visiting the websites below:

- Greyhound Adoption Program NSW: www.gapnsw.org.au
- Greyhounds as Pets (NSW): www.thedogs.com.au
- Greyhound Adoption Program Victoria: www.gap.grv.org.au
- Greyhound Adoption Program South Australia: www.gapsa.org.au
- Greyhound Adoption Program of Queensland: www.greyhoundpets.org.au
- Greyhounds as pets Western Australia: www.greyhoundsaspets.com.au

RSPCA

Animal

Tales

RSPCA
Animal Tales
A New Home for Cocoa
Buying this book helps the RSPCA look after animals!
Helen Kelly

RSPCA
Animal Tales
Florence Takes the Lead
Buying this book helps the RSPCA look after animals!